muma I can read!

Stories by Jyoti Bansal

First Published in April 2019

ISBN: 978-93-5347-368-6

Price: INR 350/-

BLUE ROSE PUBLISHERS

www.bluerosepublishers.com

info@bluerosepublishers.com

+91 8882 898 898

Cover Design:
Mohit Joshi

Typographic Design:
Namrata Saini

Distributed by: Blue Rose, Amazon, Flipkart, Shopclues

For my boys who inspire me always

Tanush and **Namish**

Contents

Illustrations by....

Kasheeka Vig
Jyoti Bansal

Ice Cream

It's a happy sunny day, as Vana's mom promised to take her to the ice cream shop today!

So when Vana came from her school, she wore her blue jeans and her favorite tshirt. She held her mom's hand. Both walked in to the icecream shop.

Vana ashed for a bubble gum flavor in her favorite chocolate cone.

She licked her ice cream. Her mom smiled as she love to see her happy.

Teddy

Teddy and I are best buddies. We eat, sleep, giggle, bath together....

My Dad gave me Teddy when I was a baby. I love its cute little orange bow on its neck.

It hugs me when I am sad. It is soft and cuddly.

One day I went shopping with Mom and when I came home my Teddy was nowhere! I was so sad.

But mom found it in the shopping bag. I gave it a hug and told Teddy that I will never loose it again.

Bed Time

Its bed me for Vana and Sam. Sam closes his bedroom curtains. Then bush his teeth. Vana puts on her pyjamas. She jumps into her bed. She calls Sam. But cant hear him. " Where is he?" She thinks.

Behind the curtain?....... No, under the bed !!.......... No !

Then she saw sweet little Sam slept on the rug near his toy.

Grandma Puppy

I take care of the puppy with my grandma. She shows me how to care for the puppy. I put water in its dish and some food in a pan we got for it. The puppy likes the water and the dog food.

The puppy plays with me inside and outside the house the whole day. It runs to look for the ball I throw. After we play, the puppy and I take a nap.

Got Hurt

Sam was playing with a ball out in the garden with Vana and Tom. Sam kicked so hard he fell.

He cried so loud, his mom, uncle,all friends came to see. " Oh! You got hurt Sam, his uncle said.

His Mom picked him up in her arms and said " it's a tiny little scratch Sam!" she cleaned it, kissed him on his cheek. Sam smiled and ran again to play.

The New Bicycle

Vana has a new bicycle. It is pink and very shiny. It was a gift her Mom gave her. She hid it behind a bush to surprise her.

When Vana looked behind the bush and saw the bicycle, she jumped for joy. It was just what she wanted. She gave her Mom a big hug. She loves her new bicycle and her Mom too.

Mr. Frog

Vana saw a frog in a pond. The frog was green in color.

The frog liked to jump up and down. It jumped in the pond and 'splash' came the water on Vana's face.

She called the frog near her.... Then she picked the frog in her hand and smiled at it.

They played together all day long. Then Vana went home to tell her stories and about her new friend to her Mom.

A day in Snow

Sam and Vana are very happy. There is lots of snow for them to play. Sam gets his fur coat and Vana pulls up her boots. She gets her red sled. They both go up the hill and the come down in their sled.

"This is so much fun" says Sam.

"Do you want to go up again Sam?" asks Vana.

"Yes! Lets do it again," says Sam.

They both go up and come down the hill on the sled till it gets dark.

It was a fun day in snow for both.

In a Restaurant

You can go to a restaurant to eat breakfast, lunch or dinner and even a snack when you want.

Restaurant serves food to you and to other people who go and eat at their place.

First, you look at the menu that lists all of the foods and drinks that you can order from the restaurant. Then you tell the waiter what you want to eat and drink. They bring you your order.

When you have finished you pay them the bill and say Thank you for yummy food.

The Dentist

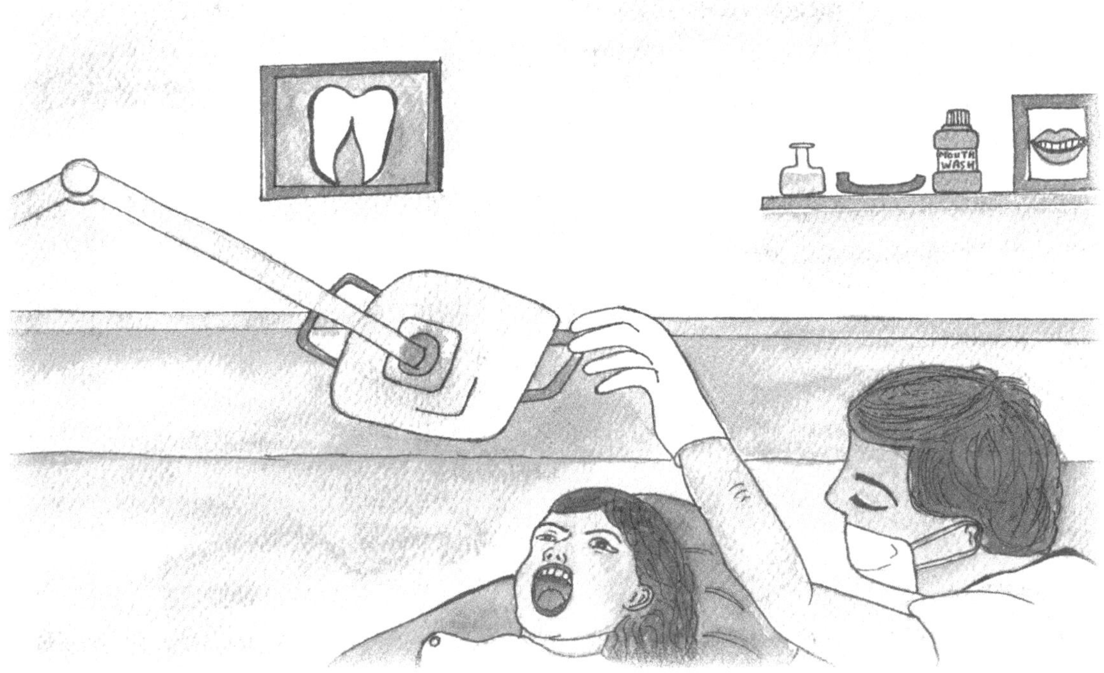

The dentist takes care of your teeth. Are you clean? The dentist wants you to use your toothbrush everyday.

Brushing your teeth will keep them strong, healthy and shiny.

The dentist has tools to clean your teeth and to check if you have any cavity.

After he is done, he sends you home saying you doing well. He is very nice.

The Thunderstorm

The kids were outside playing catch. They heard a rumble in the sky.

They didn't want to stop playing but Mom called them in. she said it was not safe to play outside as it will rain.

They all decided to go inside and play a game. They loved listening to the thunder as they played their game.

The kids went outside again after the storm had passed. They got amazed when they saw a big rainbow.

Homework or Video Games

Sam loves to play video games. His favorites are car games.

Sam got home from school one day. His mom asked him if he had any homework. He did have but he said no to his mom, as he wanted to play with video games.

Then he changed his mind. He did not want to tell a lie to his mother, as it was a bad thing.

So he did his homework first and played two games before dinner. He knows it is best to be honest.

The Puppy and The Kitten

My family got a puppy and a kitten from the animal shelter. They were so young and small; they did not even have names yet. We had to think of good names for them.

The puppy likes to jump up the whole day. The kitten likes to curl up in our laps.

"What do you want to name them?" asked Mom.

My sister said," Jumpy for the puppy and Cuddles for the kitten".

We all loved those names.

At the Zoo

I went to the zoo with my friends.

First I saw the white bear, and then I saw the black.

Then I saw the camel with a hump upon his back.

Then I saw the worm wiggle in the grass.

Then I saw the grey wolf, with mutton in his mouth.

Then I saw the Elephant waving his truck high up in the air.

Then I saw the monkeys, mercy! How unpleasantly they smell.

Baking Day

Today Sam and Vana will bake a chocolate cake with Mom at home.

She needs help in mixing the eggs and butter first. Sam loves to stir and Vana loves to lick the spoon with chocolate mixture on it.

Mom got a new teddy shape baking mold. Kids love it.

Kids helped Mom to pour the mixture in the mold. Then put the mixture in the oven to bake.

Yummy, the chocolate cake is ready in no time.

www.ingramcontent.com/pod-product-compliance
Ingram Content Group UK Ltd.
Pitfield, Milton Keynes, MK11 3LW, UK
UKHW061826190726
13853UKWH00009B/2452